About Mules

Imagine if a horse and a donkey had a baby. Well, that baby would be called a mule. Mules don't like being made to do anything unless they want to. They're very stubborn creatures, just like some people! But mules are clever and they're easy to train if you treat them kindly. If you ever meet a mule, be sure to be gentle. Then he'll want to be your friend. He'll have lots of fun playing with you. And he'll forget all about being stubborn!

For my friend David Fenton,

and for my friend Derek Whitehead.

Thank you for always being such great supporters.

With love —P.D.E.

To the dear Nicolo —B.N.

Henry Holt and Company, LLC
Publishers since 1866
115 West 18th Street
New York, New York 10011
www.henryholt.com

Henry Holt is a registered trademark of Henry Holt and Company, LLC

Text copyright © 2002 by Pamela Duncan Edwards
Illustrations copyright © 2002 by Barbara Nascimbeni
All rights reserved.
First published in the United States in 2002 by Henry Holt and Company, LLC.
Originally published in the United Kingdom in 2002 by Macmillan Children's Books,
a division of Macmillan Publishers Limited, under the title *"Won't!"said Mule*.

Library of Congress Cataloging-in-Publication Data
Edwards, Pamela Duncan.
Rude mule / Pamela Duncan Edwards; illustrated by Barbara Nascimbeni.
Originally published: United Kingdom: Macmillan Children's Books, 2002.
Summary: A rude mule learns that he has more fun when he uses good manners.
[1. Mules—Fiction. 2. Behavior—Fiction. 3. Etiquette—Fiction.]
I. Nascimbeni, Barbara, ill. II. Title.
PZ7.E26365 Ru 2002 [E]—dc21 2001004628

ISBN 0-8050-7007-9 / First American Edition—2002
Printed in Belgium
1 3 5 7 9 10 8 6 4 2

PAMELA DUNCAN EDWARDS

Rude Mule

Illustrated by
BARBARA NASCIMBENI

HENRY HOLT AND COMPANY
NEW YORK

What would you do
if a mule knocked on your door one day
and said "I've come for lunch"?
You'd say, "Hello! Come in, Mule."

What if he came in and sat down at the table?

You'd say, "Mule, wash your hooves before lunch."

But what if he said "Won't!"

You'd say, "No lunch for you, then."

What if he brayed a rude mule hee-haw?

You'd ignore him until he stopped, wouldn't you?

What if he got tired of making a fuss and
washed his hooves under the tap politely?
You'd say, "Would you like some spaghetti?"
What if he just said "Okay"?
You'd say, "Mule, say, 'Yes, please.'"

What if he said "Won't!"?
You'd say, "No spaghetti for you, then."

What if he brayed a rude mule hee-haw
and stamped his four stubborn hooves?
You'd ignore him until he stopped,
wouldn't you?

What if he got tired of making a fuss and said
"Yes, please" politely?

You'd serve him some spaghetti, wouldn't you?

And what if he began to slurp and gobble?

You'd say, "Mule, eat your food quietly."

But what if he said "Won't!"?

You'd say, "Then we won't be able to play
with my train set after lunch."

What if he brayed a rude mule hee-haw
and stamped his four stubborn hooves and
blew a loud "plaaah" down his big mule nose?

plaaah!

You'd ignore him until
he stopped, wouldn't you?

What if he got tired of making a fuss
and began to eat quietly?
You'd say, "When we play with my train set,
you can be the driver."

But what if he got very excited
and jumped down from his chair?
You'd say, "Mule, ask, 'May I leave the table?'"
What if he said "Won't!"?
You'd say, "Then my train will have to do
without a driver today."

What if he brayed a rude mule hee-haw
and stamped his four stubborn hooves
and blew a loud "plaaah" down his big mule
nose and poked out his red mule tongue?
You'd ignore him until he stopped,
wouldn't you?

What if he got tired of making a fuss
and said "Please may I leave the table?"
very politely?

Then Mule would get to drive the train.

You'd play hide-and-seek.

What if he said "I'm going home now!"
and got ready to leave?
You'd say, "Mule, what should you say now?"
What if he blinked his bright mule eyes
and wrinkled his mule forehead and thought
and thought?

Then what if he smiled a big toothy mule smile
and said very politely "Thank you for having me.
I've had a lovely time"?
You'd say, "Come again tomorrow and
we'll paddle in my wading pool."

Then I bet he'd bray
a happy mule hee-haw

and clap his mule hooves
and blow a quiet "plaaah"
down his big mule nose

and lick you gently with his red mule tongue

and give you
a giant mule hug.

Then you'd wave good-bye to him
very politely.

And you'd go and get your wading pool ready,
wouldn't you?

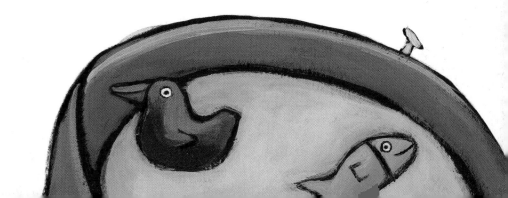